A SCIENCE

The Magic School Bus
CHAPTER BOOK

THE FISHY FIELD TRIP

Join my class on all of our Magic School Bus adventures!

A SCIENCE

The Magic School Bus

CHAPTER BOOK

THE FISHY FIELD TRIP

SCHOLASTIC INC.

New York   Toronto   London   Auckland   Sydney
Mexico City   New Delhi   Hong Kong   Buenos Aires

Written by Martin Schwabacher.

Illustrations by Hope Gangloff.

Based on *The Magic School Bus* books
written by Joanna Cole and illustrated by Bruce Degen.

The author would like to thank Douglas Fenner, PhD,
of the Australian Institute of Marine Science,
for his expert advice in preparing this manuscript.

No part of this publication may be reproduced in whole or in part, or stored in a retrieval system, or transmitted in any form or by any means, electronic, mechanical, photocopying, recording, or otherwise, without written permission of the publisher. For information regarding permission, write to Scholastic Inc., Attention: Permissions Department, 557 Broadway, New York, NY 10012.

ISBN 0-439-56052-7

24 23 22 21 20 19 18   10 11 12 13 14 15 16/0

Designed by Louise Bova

Printed in the U.S.A.   40

First printing, March 2004

A SCIENCE

The Magic School Bus
CHAPTER BOOK

THE FISHY FIELD TRIP

◄❚►INTRODUCTION◄❚►

Hi. My name is Tim. I am one of the kids in Ms. Frizzle's class.

Maybe you've heard of Ms. Frizzle. (Sometimes we just call her the Friz.) She is a terrific teacher — as long as you're not afraid of a little adventure. The Friz is a wiz in science, and she'll do just about anything to teach us about it.

When the Friz takes us on field trips on the Magic School Bus, we see some pretty amazing things. Believe me, it's not called *magic* for nothing! Once you step on that bus, anything can happen.

Ms. Frizzle likes to surprise us, but we can usually tell when she is planning a special lesson — we just look at what she's wearing.

The other day, Ms. Frizzle came to school wearing a dress covered with tropical fish. At first I didn't think anything of it, since we'd been studying the ocean all week. I should have known from looking at her dress that we were about to plunge into the adventure of our lives.

CHAPTER 1

"Look! There are some new fish in the tank!" Phoebe shouted. Everyone gathered around the big fish tank that Ms. Frizzle had brought in for Ocean Awareness Day.

"Wow! Check out the stripes on that angelfish," Ralphie said. "I drew one of those for my coral reef report."

Everyone crowded around to look at the bright blue-and-yellow fish. But I couldn't keep my eyes from wandering to the shelf above. There it was — the big, beautiful book on coral reefs that our class had been working on together for days.

"That picture you painted for the cover is awesome, Tim," Carlos said.

"Thanks, Carlos," I said. I'd spent two days drawing a coral reef, and it had turned out pretty well. "I think your shark pictures are great, too."

"Thanks!" he said. "This was one art project I could really sink my teeth into — but for a while, I was afraid I'd bitten off more than I could chew."

Coral Reefs
by Ralphie

Coral reefs are rocky structures built by tiny animals called corals. The reefs grow only in warm, shallow, tropical waters. Although coral reefs cover just a small fraction of the ocean floor, they are home to about a third of all ocean fish species.

I rolled my eyes as Carlos made biting motions, imitating a shark.

"Is everyone ready, class?" Ms. Frizzle said. "Tonight is the big night."

I swallowed hard. That evening, the whole school was having a big assembly for Ocean Awareness Day. Our class was going to present our special handmade book on coral reefs. We each had to get up and talk about our drawings and reports.

I was a little nervous, and not just about talking in front of the whole school and everybody's parents. My aunt Joanne would be visiting from San Francisco. She's a professional children's book artist and had always encouraged me to draw, too. I really wanted the assembly to go well.

"Why don't we have one last rehearsal," the Friz said. She smiled at me. "Could you bring us the book, please, Tim?"

"Okay," I said.

But as I reached for the book, Liz, our class lizard, jumped up next to it. She swung her tail, trying to balance herself — and knocked the book right off the shelf.

"No!" I shouted.

I lunged for the book, but it was too late. With a giant splash, it fell right into the fish tank!

In a flash, I reached into the water and pulled it out. All of our hand-painted artwork was totally soaked.

Keesha ran to get some paper towels to pat it dry, but it was too late. My cover painting was nothing but a swirling mass of wet paint. We flipped through the book to check the other pictures. They were all destroyed, too.

"It's ruined!" I said. "What are we going to do now?"

"Maybe we can still give our reports without the pictures," Dorothy Ann said.

Arnold pointed at the dripping book. "Not me," he said mournfully. "My whole report was in there."

"Mine, too," I said. I flipped to the pages I had filled with information about coral reef animals. The ink was hopelessly blurred.

"Don't worry, class!" said Ms. Frizzle. "A little water won't ruin Ocean Awareness Day!"

"But what about all our pictures — and our research? They're gone," Wanda said. "How will we give our presentation without that book?"

"We'll make another one, of course!" Ms. Frizzle said.

I couldn't figure out why she looked so pleased. I had spent all week working on those pictures! "I don't think I could do all that research again in one day," I said.

"Sure you can — if we go right to the source," said Ms. Frizzle.

"Uh-oh. I think I see where this is going," Arnold said.

"To the bus!" Ms. Frizzle exclaimed.

"Are we going to see a real coral reef?" said Carlos. "Cool!"

"Or maybe just an aquarium?" Arnold said hopefully.

The Friz winked. "I had something a little more splashy in mind," she said.

We ran outside and piled into the Magic

School Bus. I looked out the window in time to see the bus sprout wings.

"Buckle up and prepare for takeoff!" Ms. Frizzle shouted. With a roar of its new jet engines, the Magic School Plane soared into the sky.

"Settle in for a long ride!" said the Friz.

"I knew I should have stayed home today," Arnold moaned.

·II·**CHAPTER 2**·II·

"Where are we going, anyway?" Ralphie asked.

"About as far as we can go," the Friz said cheerfully. "We're going down under!"

"You mean, underwater?" I asked.

"Underwater *and* down under," Ms. Frizzle said with a smile. "We're going somewhere truly *great*."

I knew the Friz must be hinting at something, but all I could see out the window were the clouds far below us. After a while, the drone of the engines must have made me fall asleep. I woke up with a start to hear Ms. Frizzle shouting, "We're here!"

"Huh? Where?" Ralphie asked, rubbing his eyes. I looked out the window. We were still way up above the clouds.

"The Great Barrier Reef! It's right down there," Ms. Frizzle said cheerfully.

"That's the largest coral reef area in the world!" Dorothy Ann said. "According to my notes, it's right next to Australia."

Wanda laughed. "So that's why the Friz said we were going 'down under' — that's Australia's nickname."

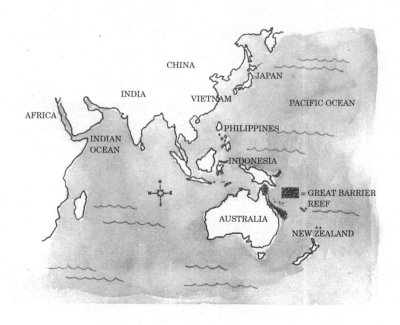

"Wow! We just went halfway around the world," Keesha said. "Cool!"

I was pretty excited myself — but I couldn't help wondering how we were ever going to get back to school in time for our presentation.

"Where are we going to land?" Carlos asked as the plane started to descend. "Jet planes can't land in the water, can they?"

"No — but birds can," said Ms. Frizzle. "Grab a feather and hold on to your hats!"

The next thing we knew, the bus had changed into a giant pelican. We had an incredible view as it glided in circles, going lower and lower. We were below the clouds now, and the water beneath us was a glorious blue.

Straight below us we could see hundreds of odd-shaped islands. "Welcome to the Great Barrier Reef," the Friz shouted. "Of course, most of it is down under — underwater, that is."

Between the islands were lots of large, light-colored patches. "What are those?" Keesha asked.

"That's the reef!" the Friz said. "All those lighter areas are huge masses of coral that don't quite reach the water's surface."

"Wow!" I said. "This goes on for miles and miles!"

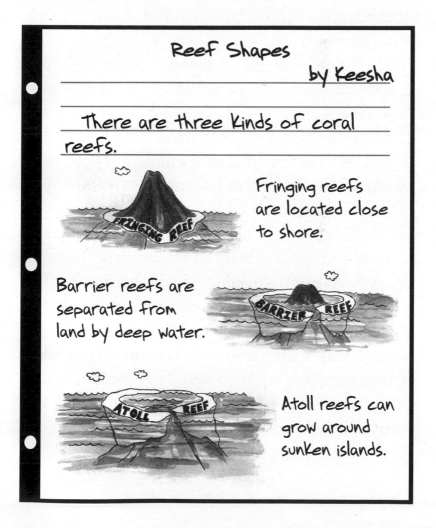

Reef Shapes
by Keesha

There are three kinds of coral reefs.

Fringing reefs are located close to shore.

Barrier reefs are separated from land by deep water.

Atoll reefs can grow around sunken islands.

"According to my research," D.A. said, "the Great Barrier Reef is actually made up of thousands of small reefs. It covers an area nearly as large as the state of California."

"Wow," Phoebe said, looking out the window. "It must have taken forever for all that coral to grow."

"What do you mean, grow?" Carlos asked. "You make it sound like coral reefs are alive."

"Oh, they are!" said Ms. Frizzle. "Don't forget, all these miles and miles of reefs were made by living animals called corals. Come on — let's get a closer look."

The Magic School Pelican swooped down toward the water. "What's happening?" Arnold asked nervously. "Where is this bird going?"

We zoomed down closer and closer to the water, then landed with a big splash.

I was a little nervous about where the Friz might take us next. But I figured it couldn't be as scary as standing up in front of the school with no report to read!

The bus-pelican started to change

shape. Its feathers disappeared, and soon we were all seated on blue plastic chairs in the Magic School Boat.

"Yikes! I think there's a hole in this boat!" Arnold said, pointing at the floor. "I can see fish down there!"

Ms. Frizzle laughed. "Don't worry, Arnold. The boat has a glass bottom so we can see what's underneath us."

We all looked down into the water below.

At first I just saw sand. Then suddenly we were over a cluster of coral.

"Wow!" said Carlos. "It's even more beautiful than the pictures."

Below us was a magical landscape unlike anything I'd ever seen. It looked like a forest of colorful enchanted rocks. Some forked up like antlers. Others looked like big clusters of bubbles.

"Hey, I know what those are!" Ralphie shouted. "I did my report on the different types of coral." He started scribbling in his notebook.

"Do you remember all their names?" Phoebe asked.

"No way — there are more than 700 kinds of corals that help build reefs," Ralphie said. "But I do know some of them. See the ones that look like big flowers? Those are called daisy coral."

"And I suppose those ones that look like big mushrooms are called mushroom corals?" Carlos joked.

"Actually, they are!" said Ralphie. "A lot of corals are named for how they look — like antler coral, finger coral, bubble coral, and grape coral."

"Ugh! What's that?" Phoebe interrupted. "It looks like a giant brain!" We looked where she was pointing.

"That's brain coral," Ralphie said. "Weird, huh?"

The brain coral looked like a giant ball covered with wrinkled ridges, just like pictures I'd seen of the human brain. Ralphie started drawing it for his report.

None of the corals looked smooth. They were all covered with little bumps and ridges. And swimming among them were swirling masses of fish, all in wild, bright colors. It was like being inside a kaleidoscope.

Crazy Corals
by Ralphie

Often you can identify coral by its shape. Here are three kinds:

Staghorn coral

Bubble coral

Brain coral

The same kind of coral can appear in several different colors.

"I can't believe how many fish there are down here!" I said. Everywhere I looked, there were more fish. There must have been thousands.

A school of small orange fish swam past. Suddenly, they all changed direction and whirled away, like leaves blowing in the wind.

"According to my research, more than 1,500 different kinds of fish live in the Great Barrier Reef," said D.A.

"Wow, look at those colors," said Wanda. "Their spots and stripes are even brighter than in the books. I wish I knew what all these fish are called."

"Those flat, yellow-and-black-striped ones are called butterfly fish," Phoebe said. "I did a report on those. And those black ones with white spots are called triggerfish." She started drawing happily. "You were right, Ms. Frizzle. I'll be able to do my report again easily down here!"

I had been so caught up in all the amazing stuff I was seeing that I had almost forgotten my reports. But unlike Phoebe and

Ralphie, I wasn't recognizing anything at all. I tried to remember what my pictures were about, but it seemed my mind had gone blank when our book fell in the fish tank.

The boat passed over the coral patch, and suddenly we were over bare sand: no coral, no fish, no plants, nothing.

"Where did all the fish go?" Ralphie asked.

"Class, this is a good lesson in how important coral is," said Ms. Frizzle. "All the fish and other animals we were seeing depend on the coral reef for protection, shelter, and food." We passed over another patch of coral, and it was crammed with life. Everything was overlapping everything else, with fish, crabs, and other animals all squeezed into the cracks.

"How does the reef provide all that?" asked Carlos.

"Small animals come to hide in the coral, and plants grow on top of it," said the Friz. "Fish come to eat the small animals and plants. Their droppings fertilize the reef even more. Before you know it, there's a whole community. But none of it would be here without the coral."

"So what do the corals eat?" asked Arnold.

"Good question!" said Ms. Frizzle. "Corals are animals — but they get food from sunlight, just like plants."

"How do they do that?" asked Carlos.

"Let's take a closer look," said the Friz. She pulled a lever on the bus-boat. With a splash, we were underwater, swimming around inside the Magic School Fish!

At first, the other fish scattered when they saw us approach. But we kept shrinking and shrinking until we were small enough that they ignored us. Then we got so small that instead of swimming away, they started looking at us like they thought we were food.

"I liked our old size better," said Arnold nervously.

"We never shrank this small at my old school," Phoebe added.

A beautiful angelfish swam by my window. It was no bigger than the ones in our tank back at school, but now it seemed as big as an elephant. And it was coming right at us!

"Help! It's going to attack!" Ralphie screamed.

"Don't worry," said Ms. Frizzle. "Coral reefs are full of good places to hide. That's how small fish like us survive." We scooted into a crack between two pieces of coral, where the bigger fish couldn't reach us.

"Hey, this coral sure is lumpy!" said Carlos.

Sure enough, now that we were close to the coral, we could see that it was covered in tiny bumps.

"That's right, Carlos. Each of those bumps is called a coral polyp," the Friz said. "Those are the living coral animals."

"I thought those big rocky things were the coral," I said, as our bus-fish wove through a maze of staghorn coral.

"In a way, they are — those rocky parts are the coral polyps' skeletons," said the Friz. "Each polyp makes a little cup of limestone to live in. Thousands of polyps build up thousands of these tiny cups, creating a piece of coral. The polyps all live on the coral skeleton's outer surface."

"I still don't see why you call it a coral *skeleton*," Wanda said.

"Well, it's not like our skeleton, of course. Our skeletons are inside our bodies, and theirs are outside," said the Friz. "The coral skeleton is a hard, bony structure that supports the polyps' soft bodies from underneath."

We zoomed in close to look at the bumpy surface of the coral. The orangish polyps were packed so close together that you couldn't even see the limestone skeleton underneath.

"Wow. Corals are more complicated than I thought," I said.

"That's not all. Look closely at those polyps," said Ms. Frizzle. "What do you see?"

Our tiny bus-fish shrank even more until we were smaller than a polyp.

"Hey — the polyps are clear!" said Carlos.

"Yeah — all their color comes from those little blobs inside," I said. "What are those?"

From the Desk of Ms. Frizzle

The rocky surfaces of coral reefs are blanketed with coral animals called polyps. On healthy reefs, thousands of polyps cover the reef like a living carpet.

Each polyp has a ring of tentacles around a cuplike mouth. During the day, the tentacles close up like a tight fist.

At night, the polyps' tentacles fill with water and get much longer, until there's a ring of long, armlike tentacles sticking out, like petals on a flower.

The polyps are closed during the day, and open at night.

"That, class, is what I call a beautiful partnership," said the Friz. "Those little brownish balls inside the polyps are tiny one-celled plants called algae."

"You mean corals have plants *inside* them?" I said. "And those plants make the corals' food?"

"Exactly!" said the Friz.

"Is that why corals live in clear, sunlit water?" said Keesha. "So the algae can grow?"

"That's right," said the Friz. "It's also why corals grow upward, toward the water's surface. And it's why coral polyps are clear — so the algae inside them can soak up the maximum amount of sunlight."

"That sounds sort of creepy. Imagine having algae living inside you," said Phoebe.

"They should toss those freeloaders out!" said Carlos.

Ms. Frizzle laughed. "No way. Those little algae are the best friends a coral could have," she said. "Like all plants, they use energy from sunlight to make food — and they share that food with the corals. Corals with algae inside them get about nine-tenths of their food from the algae!"

"That is a good partnership," I said. "The algae get a safe, sheltered home, and the corals get a steady supply of food. Not bad."

"But what if something eats the coral?" Arnold asked.

From the Desk of Ms. Frizzle

Plants of the Sea

Algae (pronounced like the name "Al" and the letter "Gee") are simple plants with no leaves, stems, roots, flowers, or seeds. But they are the main form of plant life in the ocean and the biggest source of food for ocean animals.

Algae range in size from tiny specks so small you can't even see them to huge seaweeds. They make food from sunlight through a process called photosynthesis, just like plants on land.

"Oh, come on. What could do that?" I asked. "Coral skeletons are made of limestone. It's hard as rock. It would take something with superstrong jaws to crunch up all that coral."

"Something like . . . that?" said Ralphie, pointing out the window.

A monstrous fish was cruising toward us. It was about four feet long and had a huge beak, like a giant parrot. We watched in horror as its powerful jaws opened. Then it bit a piece of coral right off! Boy, was I glad it wasn't the piece of coral we were hiding in.

There was a huge crunching sound as the fish chewed up the coral rock, so loud it hurt my ears. The big fish was moving slowly, taking its time — but now it was swimming straight at our bus-fish.

"How exciting!" said Ms. Frizzle. "You're seeing a humphead parrot fish in action! What a treat!"

The parrot fish took another huge chomp of coral from right next to us, and the whole Magic School Fish shook. We could hear and feel the crunching and chewing getting louder and louder. We were so small, the big fish couldn't see us, but that didn't make me feel any safer. Suddenly, hiding between two branches of coral didn't seem like such a good idea. We were safe from most fish — but not ones that ate coral!

"But why is it eating the coral skeleton?" D.A. asked. "It's like eating rock!"

"That's how it gets the coral animals — and the algae," said the Friz.

"So it grinds up rocks just to eat the stuff living on it?" I said. "What happens to all that rock?"

Carlos pointed to the fish. A puff of white sand came out of the back. "Oh," I said.

"Parrot fish can chew up a ton of coral in a year," said the Friz. "That makes a lot of sand. Ever wonder why the beaches are so full of white sand in Australia, Florida, and the Caribbean? A lot of that sand is coral ground up by parrot fish — though waves and storms do some of the grinding, too."

"Um, Ms. Frizzle?" said Arnold, pointing

out the window. "If we don't get out of here, we'll be ground up, too."

I watched in horror as the parrot fish opened wide and started to close its giant beak around us.

·‹‹I I›· CHAPTER 3 ·‹‹I I›·

The Friz pulled a lever, and our tiny bus-fish zoomed away just in time, as the powerful jaws of the parrot fish snapped shut behind us. Looking back, we could see the coral we'd been hiding in getting crushed into dust. The parrot fish didn't even notice us; it just kept munching.

"Whew!" I said. Our bus-fish grew back to normal fish size so we could continue our tour of the reef.

All around us, every surface seemed to be alive and wiggling with the current. Fish flitted away as we approached, while snails, slugs, and tiny crabs ignored us and searched for things to eat. We wandered through the reef, sticking close to the coral so we'd have a place to hide if necessary, until we came to a patch of green fuzzy stuff.

"What kind of coral is that?" Phoebe asked.

"That's not coral — that's algae," said the Friz. "Not the very, very small kind that lives inside coral, though. This algae is a kind of seaweed."

"But what is the algae growing on? Isn't that coral?" Carlos asked.

"The algae grows on it, yes — but not in it," the Friz replied. "This kind of algae is actually bad for coral. It can grow over a reef and choke the coral polyps."

"You mean that's killer algae?" said Keesha.

"It can be. It's usually not a problem, though, because fish eat the algae, so there's a healthy balance," said the Friz. "But if there aren't enough fish left to eat the algae, the algae can grow out of control and kill the corals."

"There's plenty of fish here," I said. "So how come this one patch of algae grew so tall?"

"Look out!" Phoebe called. A small blue fish was racing toward us — and it looked mad. It started nipping at the bus-fish's fins like a guard dog. The fish clearly wanted us to go away — and it wasn't going to take no for an answer.

"What's its problem?" I said, as our bus-fish turned tail and sped away. "We didn't do anything. And it can't be trying to eat us — it's smaller than we are!"

When we were a safe distance away, we turned back around to watch.

"That's a damselfish — also known as a farmer fish," Wanda said. "It was just guarding its algae farm. It thought we were after its crop."

"Did you say 'its farm'?" said Carlos. "You mean that fish is growing algae on purpose, like a farmer?"

"Yes!" said Wanda. "Damselfish actually raise algae for food. They'll chase away anything that tries to eat it — even fish much bigger than themselves. I did my report on damselfish. But I never thought I'd see one in action!" She started writing rapidly in her notebook.

Farmer Fish
by Wanda

Damselfish raise patches of green, fluffy algae for food. Most of their food comes from the algae they grow in their private gardens.

A damselfish starts its garden by nibbling the polyps off a patch of coral rock to clear space for the algae. As its crops grow, the damselfish weeds out algae that isn't the kind it wants.

Lots of other animals want to eat their algae, so damselfish fight fiercely to protect their turf.

We watched as a small crab crawled over the coral to pluck some algae and the damselfish shooed it away. Then it swam over to an animal that looked like a small pincushion. "Watch this," said Wanda. "It's going after that sea urchin!"

My mouth dropped open in surprise as the little damselfish picked up the sea urchin by its spines, dragged it off the coral reef, and dumped it. Then the fish went after another sea urchin and started breaking off its long, black spines! It sure was tough! But then, suddenly, the damselfish stopped and turned around.

"Uh-oh — here comes trouble," said Phoebe.

A whole gang of bright blue-and-yellow fish swooped down on the damselfish's garden. The damselfish flitted everywhere, nipping at the intruders, but it couldn't fight them all at once. The blue-and-yellow fish kept chomping down on the algae. The damselfish attacked furiously until the raiders finally zipped away. By then, its algae farm looked like it had been trampled by an entire class of fourth graders.

"Holy cow!" Carlos said. "What were those?"

"Surgeonfish," said Wanda. "They love algae, too. Those damselfish are pretty tough, but there's not much they can do when they're outnumbered."

"Will the damselfish starve now?" asked Keesha anxiously.

"Don't worry. Algae plants grow really fast!" said Wanda. "It will all grow back. And remember, the surgeonfish need to eat, too."

"Um, just curious — but is there any special reason they're called *surgeonfish?*" Arnold asked.

"Good question, Arnold!" Ms. Frizzle said with a grin. "Surgeonfish get their names from the two sharp blades on their sides, just in front of their tails. They can slice right into other fish — or into a person, if you're not careful."

"Really? Where? I don't see any blades," Carlos said, pressing his nose to the window.

"They're folded up, like a switchblade," said the Friz. "If you want to see their blades, we'll have to get closer."

"That's all right, really — I don't need to see the blades," Arnold said hurriedly.

"Watch what happens when it thinks we're going to attack it," Ms. Frizzle said, her voice filled with excitement.

We edged closer to the surgeonfish, and suddenly two blades popped out of its sides near the tail.

"Did you see that? Incredible, isn't it?" said the Friz.

Suddenly, the surgeonfish swung its tail toward us, and a hard, sharp blade scraped against our window.

We all screamed. The surgeonfish flicked its tail at us again, and I could see the sharp, shiny points on the blades.

"What are those things made of, anyway?" I asked.

"They're spines, like the ones in its fins," Wanda said, "only these are as sharp as razor blades."

"I'm glad we're in here, not out there," I said. "I wouldn't want to see them any closer."

"Me, neither," said Wanda. "Those blades could definitely slice a person's flesh."

"I sure hope they can't slice through school bus windows because here it comes again," said Ralphie.

"Well, I guess we really should be moving on," the Friz said reluctantly. Our bus-fish swam off, and when we looked back, the surgeonfish had calmed down again.

"Whew. For a second there, I thought we were *fin*-ished," Carlos said. Everyone groaned.

As we continued our tour through the reef, I noticed there were a lot more animals there than just corals and fish. I saw colorful crabs, shrimps, starfish, and lots of very pretty shells.

"Boy, it's like Halloween down here," Carlos said. I knew what he meant. Many of the creatures we were passing looked like versions of animals I had seen before, but dressed in bright costumes. Ms. Frizzle pointed out a reef lobster, which looked like a regular lobster, except its white shell was covered with lavender spots.

Then we saw some harlequin shrimps, which looked like small crabs dressed as polka-dotted clowns.

Suddenly, I saw something I recognized. "Hey! I know what those are," I said, pointing at what looked like a bush waving in the breeze. "Those are called sea fans. They're a kind of coral." All the information from my report suddenly came flooding back to me. I had drawn the sea fans after seeing a photograph of their hundreds of colorful branching arms. I couldn't wait to draw them again. My new picture would be ten times better after seeing the sea fans alive and moving.

"Those are corals?" said Wanda. "They don't look like the corals we saw before."

"Those were hard corals," I said "Sea fans are soft corals. They don't make limestone reefs, like hard corals. They have skeletons inside their bodies instead."

"They look softer, all right," said Carlos. "They're swishing around like plants."

We cruised up to a pink sea fan. Its branches waved with the current.

"Why is it so flat?" Keesha asked.

"It works like a net," I said. "Water passes through it, but the stuff floating in the water gets caught in the branches."

"You mean it's a trap?" Ralphie asked.

I nodded.

The current pushed us closer toward the sea fan. Arnold gulped nervously.

"Many sea fans are called gorgonians," the Friz said cheerfully, ignoring the danger. "They're named after a snake-haired monster from a Greek myth. Can anyone guess why these pretty little sea fans are named after a monster?" she asked.

"Well, for one thing, each of those branches has a deadly stinger on it," I said. "But shouldn't we —"

"Excellent!" said Ms. Frizzle. "Good work, Tim."

"Um — if it's such a deadly monster, do we have to get so close?" Arnold asked.

"How else will we see it eat?" Ms. Frizzle answered. I held my breath as she steered the bus-fish closer to the sea fan.

As we got closer, we were amazed to see a bunch of skinny animals shaped like stars with their arms wound around the branches.

"Is the sea fan eating those star animals?" I asked.

Ms. Frizzle shook her head. "The sea fan is not really dangerous to bigger animals," she said. "It eats mostly teeny, tiny floating things called plankton. Those brittle stars live right up there on the sea fan, where they can catch plankton, too."

Tons and Tons of Plankton
by Phoebe

A single teaspoon of ocean water contains thousands of animals and plants. These tiny, one-celled creatures are called plankton. They are so plentiful that many ocean animals eat nothing else.

I peered closer at the sea fan. I was almost disappointed that it wasn't more deadly.

"I thought Tim said their branches can sting," Ralphie said.

"They can," said the Friz, "but the stingers are mostly for catching plankton, not big fish like us. The sea fans don't contain algae, so they catch plankton for food. This species' stingers aren't that strong — not like, say, a sea anemone's."

"Did you say 'an enemy'?" Carlos asked.

"No: AN-EM-ON-E," the Friz answered. "They're animals related to corals. The stingers on their tentacles are so strong that they can kill a fish!"

"You know, we don't need to see that," said Arnold. "I think we got the idea just fine with the gorgonian."

"But we have to!" D.A. said. "My report was about clownfish."

"Yeah, a clownfish sounds great," Arnold said, perking up. "Let's look for one of those and forget the anemone."

D.A. laughed. "Sorry, Arnold," she said. "I doubt we'll see a clownfish without an anemone. They live together."

"But I thought sea anemones *killed* fish," Phoebe said.

"Most fish, yeah, but — hey, look! There's an anemone now," D.A. said. "Let's see if there's a clownfish, too!"

The sea anemone had a short, stubby body with hundreds of pink, wiggly tentacles sticking out the top. It looked like a living piece of shag carpet.

"Watch what happens when we go up close!" Ms. Frizzle said.

Arnold sighed.

We swam closer and closer until our bus-fish touched the sea anemone's tentacles — and suddenly they grabbed us!

◄◊► CHAPTER 4 ◄◊►

Through the windows of the bus-fish, I could see the sea anemone's pink tentacles closing around us. It was like we were being gripped by a hundred-fingered hand — and the fingers had glue on them.

The Magic School Fish strained and struggled to pull away, but the tentacles just stretched without letting go. More and more tentacles closed around us until they covered the whole window.

"It's a good thing we're a bus-fish, not a real fish, or those stingers would have already finished us off," D.A. said. But somehow that didn't make me feel too lucky. We were still trapped.

Finally, Ms. Frizzle flipped a lever, and the bus-fish roared into action. One by one, the anemone's tentacles lost their grip and had to let go. At last we tore loose, and everybody cheered.

"Whoopie! Wasn't that exciting, kids?" Ms. Frizzle said. "Want to do it again?"

"No!" we all shouted. We circled back toward the anemone, but this time we stayed a safe distance away.

"That's how the sea anemone eats," the Friz explained. "There's a kind of mouth in the middle, where it pulls in its prey. After being stung by those tentacles, most other animals couldn't struggle free like we did."

"You mean, the anemone was trying to eat us?" Arnold gulped.

"Oh, yes," said the Friz. "Each tentacle has thousands of stinging cells that shoot out tiny needles full of venom. Good thing they couldn't reach us in here, eh?"

"We never had poison needles shot at us in my old school," Phoebe said.

"Look!" shouted D.A. "There's a clown-fish!"

To our amazement, a funny-looking orange-and-white fish was nestled among the anemone's tentacles, totally unharmed.

"How come it's not getting hurt?" I asked.

"The clownfish is coated with slimy mucus, so the anemone can't sting it," said D.A. "That's where the clownfish lives — right there with the anemone."

"Yuck! Why would it live there?" Ralphie asked.

"For protection, mainly," she said. "The anemone is like the clownfish's personal body-guard. Also, it gets to eat part of what the anemone catches."

"A clownfish sounds like a real pest, living with the anemone and eating its food," said Carlos.

"Not at all," said D.A. "They both help each other because the clownfish chases away the anemone's enemies."

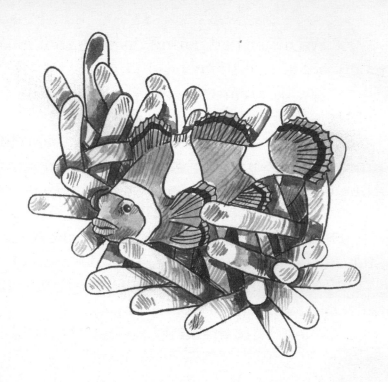

"It's a classic case of mutualism because both sides benefit," added Ms. Frizzle.

"Like the coral with the algae inside it?" I said.

"Exactly!" said Ms. Frizzle. "Symbiotic relationships can occur anywhere, but they're especially common here. Everything lives together in such close quarters on the reef that they have developed some ingenious ways to share space. See that sponge over there? You'd never believe all the things living inside it!"

"Sponges aren't alive . . . are they?" Arnold said nervously.

"Yep. Down here, sponges are animals. But they still soak up things, just like the plastic sponges in your kitchen," the Friz replied.

The bus-fish cruised over to a bright red sponge. As we came closer, we could see it was filled with holes.

"Can't you just tell us about the sponge this time, from over here?" said Arnold.

"Why tell you when I can show you?" Ms. Frizzle said.

The Magic School Fish started to shrink until it was smaller than a pea. Then the Friz turned off the engine, but we kept going forward. The closer we got to the sponge, the faster we were moving. It felt like we were being pulled toward it. I could feel the whole bus-fish start to shake.

"We're getting sucked inside!" Phoebe said.

"And away we go!" said Ms. Frizzle.

From the Desk of Ms. Frizzle

It's All Mutual

Many animals that live close together form partnerships for survival. The name for this relationship is *symbiosis*.

There are two main kinds of symbiotic relationships:

Mutualism is when both partners benefit — like sea anemones and clownfish.

Commensalism is when one benefits from the other, without helping or hurting it — like a fish that hides in coral.

We passed through one of the many openings in the sponge, and the moving water carried us into a long, winding passageway. The sides of the tunnel were lined with what looked like little hairs. They were paddling like mad to keep the water moving through the sponge.

There were small chambers all around us — and almost every one had some kind of animal living in it. It was like we had stumbled into a tiny, underwater apartment building.

Sea Sponges
by Dorothy Ann

Sponges are filter feeders – animals that pump water through their bodies and filter out tiny particles of food. That's why sponges are full of holes.

A sponge the size of a football can filter nearly a thousand gallons (3785 L) of water per day. That's enough water to fill more than twenty-five bathtubs!

There were small fish in some and crabs in others. Then we got to a section packed with tiny white things that looked like insects.

"What the heck are those?" said Phoebe. There were hundreds of them.

"A colony of shrimps!" Ms. Frizzle said. "But these are not your usual shrimps. They're all related and live together as a giant family, like a colony of bees."

"Those shrimps sure are shrimpy!" said Carlos. "They're as small as ants!"

"Why do those have bigger claws than the rest?" Ralphie asked, pointing to a group of shrimp in front of us.

"Each shrimp in the colony has a certain job," Ms. Frizzle said, "and those are the guards."

"What are they guarding against?" I asked. "It seems pretty safe in here."

"True, we're out of reach of large fish," the Friz said. "But other predators can fit in here," she said.

"Like what?" Arnold asked.

"Like that!" Keesha screamed. A bushy, bristly beast was squeezing down the passageway.

"Oh, what luck! A bristle worm," said Ms. Frizzle. "It's come to hunt. I wonder what those guards will do."

Bushy, Bristly Worms
by Arnold

Many more kinds of worms live in the ocean than live on land. More than a hundred different species of worms can sometimes be found living inside a single piece of coral!

One common type of ocean worm is the bristle worm. These worms have bushy hairs sticking out all over their bodies. There are more than 5,000 different kinds of bristle worms.

The hungry worm worked its way through the passageway, feeling around for something to eat. The closer it got to our bus-fish, the more spiny bristles we saw. Its whole body was covered with them!

Most of the smaller animals scurried away. But three guard shrimps scurried over to the worm and started nipping at its feelers with their claws. The worm started backing away.

"Hurray! They're protecting the colony," Ms. Frizzle said.

But the guards weren't done. While the bristle worm retreated, the shrimp turned and started pinching the fins of the Magic School Fish. More guards were pouring down the passageway to join the attack.

"Let's get out of here!" I yelled.

Ms. Frizzle turned the ignition key and put her foot on the gas. Our bus-fish tore loose from the claws of the guard shrimps and took off down a tunnel. The shrimps chased us until we swooped out of the sponge into open water.

"Whew," I said. "It seems like everything is trying to eat everything else down here. I'm glad that's over with."

"Um, Tim?" Carlos said. "I don't think it's exactly over." I looked in the direction he was pointing. We were face-to-face with the worst monster we'd encountered yet.

⋙ CHAPTER 5 ⋘

Just inches from my face was a bizarre animal that looked like a mutant starfish. It had about 18 legs, and its body was covered with hundreds of sharp spikes. Its skin was reddish brown, but the tips of the spikes were bloodred.

"That's a crown-of-thorns starfish!" Wanda said. "I did my report on them. It's even prettier in person!"

"Okay, I can see why it's called a crown-of-thorns," said Ralphie. "But I sure wouldn't call it pretty! Hideous is more like it."

"That's for sure," I said. "It looks like a cross between a starfish and a big, hairy spider that fell in a paint can."

"See those spines?" Wanda said. "They're poisonous!"

"That's supposed to make us like it better?" Ralphie said.

The spiny starfish was creeping slowly over a big plate-shaped coral. Behind it, the coral looked bare and white.

"What happened to that coral back there?" Keesha asked. "Why is it all white?"

"The starfish killed it," Wanda said. "Those things eat coral, but they don't go after the rocky part, just the living polyps," Wanda said. "That white area is bare, dead coral skeleton. But that's not all."

"There's more?" I said.

"Here's the really weird part," said Wanda. "To eat, the crown-of-thorns starfish pushes its stomach out through its mouth and puts it on top of the coral. Then it digests the coral, with its stomach outside of its body!"

"That's the most disgusting thing I've ever heard!" said D.A. "Tell me more!"

"It gets worse," Wanda said. "Sometimes thousands of these things show up at the same time. When they do, they can kill an entire coral reef."

"Can anything stop them?" I said.

The Friz grinned. "Watch this, Tim," she said.

We swam closer to where the monster was slowly crawling over the coral. A little crab popped up from a crevice. It stood in the path of the starfish, waving its claws defiantly. As the starfish approached, the crab clipped some of its thorns right off! Then it jabbed at the starfish's soft underbelly. The monster backed away.

"Hurray!" I shouted. "Way to go, little crab!"

"What made it stand up to the starfish like that?" Carlos asked. "Couldn't it have gotten poked with one of those poisonous spines?"

"It was protecting its home," Ms. Frizzle said. "Remember, lots of animals depend on the coral reef. The coral gives the crab a home, so the crab defends the coral."

"More mutualism!" D.A. said.

"That's right. But we haven't yet experi-

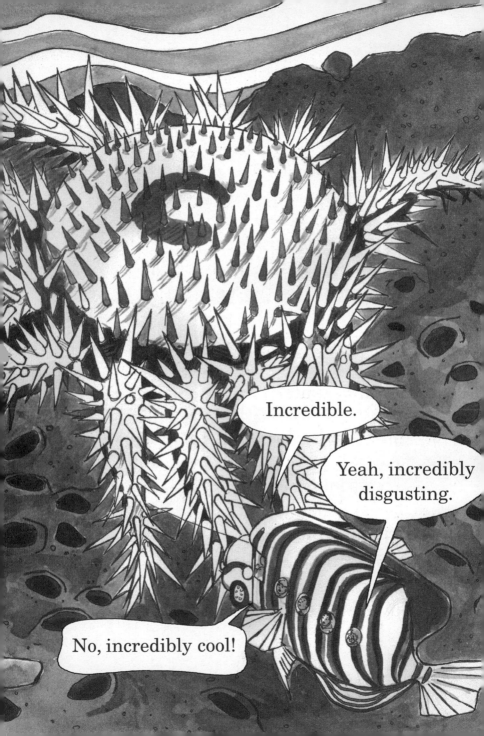

enced my favorite example of mutualism," the Friz announced. "Class, it's time to leave the bus!"

"Right here? But I can't swim!" Arnold said.

"You can now!" said the Friz.

In an instant, we were outside the bus-fish, completely surrounded by water. I looked down and saw that my arms had turned into fins, and my legs had become a tail. The Friz had turned us all into fish!

I found that by wiggling my tail from side to side, I could cruise quickly through the water. But the best part was I could now breathe underwater!

It took a few minutes to get used to it, but after that, being a fish was fantastic. I used the fins on my sides to steer, and the fin on my back to keep from rolling over. To move forward, I mostly used my tail.

"This is awesome," Carlos called out as he swooped by. I scooted around some coral and caught up to him, dodging a sea fan on the way. It was incredibly fun — like a combination between a video game and the best water-park ride in the world.

How to Breathe Underwater
by Tim

Fish can breathe underwater because they have gills instead of lungs. Gills are organs that take oxygen from water, just as lungs take oxygen from the air. To breathe, a fish opens its mouth and sucks in some water. Then it closes its mouth and pushes out the water through flaps on the side of its head. On the way out, the water flows over the gills. Oxygen from the water is absorbed into the fish's blood.

I weaved among the coral, practicing turning left and right until I could control exactly where I was going. When I wanted to cover a bigger distance, I found that a few powerful thrusts of my tail made me shoot forward really fast, and I had to brake with my side fins to slow down again.

Swimming around was really great, but I was getting more and more nervous that we wouldn't make it back in time for the assembly. I was about to say something to the Friz when Dorothy Ann swam over with a flick of her tail. "Ms. Frizzle? What exactly are we looking for?" she asked.

A Fishy Tail
by Carlos

The tail is a fish's most important fin for swimming. Fish get most of their power from pushing their tails from side to side.

The big tail muscles running down the side of a fish's body account for about half of its body weight.

I had forgotten that the whole reason we had changed into fish was to look for — I mean, "experience" — Ms. Frizzle's favorite example of mutualism.

"Gather 'round, kids," the Friz called out. "We're about to visit a cleaning station."

"A cleaning station? How could anyone get dirty in the water? We're practically in a giant bathtub!" Carlos said.

"Fish need to be cleaned regularly," Ms. Frizzle said. "They get covered with parasites — tiny little animals that live on their skin. They also have dead skin that needs to be cleaned off. And if a fish gets a cut, it needs to have it cleaned so it won't get infected."

"How can fish clean themselves?" Phoebe asked. "They don't have any arms!"

"Good question," Ms. Frizzle said. "The answer is, they get someone else to do it. Do you see those small, striped fish over there? Those are cleanerfish. They wait at special cleaning stations around the reef to clean other fish."

Next to a tall clump of coral, I could see

some small, skinny fish just a couple inches long. They were whitish, and each had a long black stripe going down the side of its body.

As we watched, a much larger fish, about ten times the size of the cleanerfish, swam up to the cleaning station. It held perfectly still.

"That's a grouper," Ms. Frizzle said. "Normally, it would eat a fish this size. But it came here to be cleaned, so it has to behave."

The cleanerfish swam right up to the grouper, completely unafraid. It began nibbling on the side of the bigger fish. The grouper didn't move a muscle.

Then the cleanerfish swam over to the grouper's mouth. The grouper opened its toothy jaws wide — and the cleanerfish swam right inside!

"Oh, no!" Phoebe cried. "It will get eaten now for sure!"

But the grouper stayed perfectly still while the tiny cleanerfish picked clean the inside of its mouth. Meanwhile, another cleanerfish swam right inside the grouper's gills. I couldn't believe it.

"What a gross job," I said. "What's in it for the cleanerfish?"

"Food!" said D.A. "The parasites and debris are the cleanerfish's lunch."

"There are cleaning stations like this all over the reef," Ms. Frizzle told us, "some with cleanerfish and some with cleaner-shrimps. Even turtles and sharks come by to get cleaned."

"Did you say sharks? Down here?" said Arnold, looking around.

"Sure," the Friz said, "but even sharks won't hurt cleanerfish. Oh, how exciting! A moray eel!"

A gigantic, serpent-shaped creature poked its head out of a hole and opened its mouth to let in a cleanerfish. I couldn't believe the cleanerfish went in there. The moray eel was huge!

"That's a black-blotched moray," Ms. Frizzle said. It was easy to see how it got its name. The eel's whole body was covered with black spots.

"Look at those fine teeth!" said Ms.

Frizzle, waving a fin at its sharp, pointed fangs. "It won't bother you if you don't bother it. But don't get too close!"

The cleanerfish went so far into the moray's mouth that we couldn't see it anymore. I started to get nervous. But then the fish swam out again, and the moray eel pulled itself back into its lair. By then, two more fish were waiting to be cleaned, including a very pretty fish with blue-and-yellow stripes and a huge lumpy fish that Wanda recognized from her report as a "potato cod."

"Get in line, kids!" Ms. Frizzle said.

"What do you mean?" I asked.

"Time to get cleaned! Follow me." She swam over behind the potato cod.

"No thanks. I just went to the dentist," said Arnold. But when everyone else got in line behind Ms. Frizzle, he took his place at the end, flitting back and forth nervously.

I was right behind Ms. Frizzle, at the front. When she opened her mouth, I did, too. Before I knew it, a little cleanerfish had swum inside. I tried to hold perfectly still. I could feel it nibbling away at my teeth, while another cleanerfish picked at my scales. It didn't hurt a bit — it just tickled.

"Ah! That feels good!" said Ms. Frizzle when she was finished. I swam over to join her, and we watched the rest of the class getting cleaned.

Before they had finished, though, Ms. Frizzle suddenly shouted, "That's enough, class — over here, quick!" She sounded like she meant it, so everyone rushed over.

"What's wrong? I was just starting to like it," Arnold said.

"Do you notice anything odd about that cleanerfish over there?" Ms. Frizzle said.

"No," I said. The fish she was pointing at looked just like all the others to me.

"Look closely at its mouth, and that longer fin on the bottom," Ms. Frizzle said. "That's not a cleanerfish. It's a false cleanerfish!"

"A what?" Keesha asked.

"It's an imposter. Just watch," the Friz said.

A big angelfish approached the cleaning station and opened its mouth. The false cleanerfish swam over, as if to pick off parasites. But then it took a bite right out of the angelfish's side! The angelfish chased after it, but quick as a flash, the trickster was gone.

"False cleanerfish look almost exactly like cleanerfish, but they're not even related," said the Friz. "Their whole appearance is a disguise. They pretend to be cleaners to get close enough to attack."

"That's awful!" Wanda said. "How could you ever trust a cleanerfish, with those imposters around?"

"Fortunately, the false ones are very rare," Ms. Frizzle said. "But you're right — with too many of those around, the whole system would break down. It's a good lesson, though: Things are not always what they seem on the reef. For instance, do you see that pile of stones over there?"

She pointed her fin at a pile of stones lying against a clump of coral. "Some of those aren't really stones. You can't tell now, but just watch." A small fish swam by the rock pile. Then, suddenly, one of the stones opened its mouth and sucked in the little fish.

"Wow! What was that?" said Keesha.

"A stonefish," said the Friz. "It's really a fish, but it looks just like a stone."

"Amazing! You can't even see it in those rocks," Wanda said. The stonefish settled back into its rock pile, where its pattern made it nearly invisible.

"That, children, is a perfect example of camouflage," said the Friz.

How to Be (Almost) Invisible
by Arnold

Many animals are the same colors as the things around them. This can help keep the animals alive because it makes them hard to see.

Hiding by blending in with your surroundings is called camouflage.

You can use camouflage in two ways. One is for protection. If a predator can't see you, it's less likely to eat you.

You can also use camouflage to launch sneak attacks, like the stonefish does. It secretly lies in wait for its victims to pass by, then gobbles them up.

"Look closely," Ms. Frizzle added, "and you'll see lots of other animals camouflaged among the coral."

Carlos and I swam over to some bright orange coral, which looked like a bunch of flowers. At first we couldn't see anything on it, but then we noticed what looked like a bright orange slug. The slug was hard to see because it was the exact same color as the coral. "Hey, look at this!" Carlos called out.

"Very good, Carlos," Ms. Frizzle said. "You found a camouflaged sea slug. It's a kind of snail, but it has no shell."

Fake Flowers
by Carlos

Orange daisy corals look a lot like flowers – and so do the sea slugs that eat them. As the sea slug eats the coral, it absorbs the coral's coloring. The slug becomes the same color as the coral, which makes it hard to see – and keeps it from being eaten itself.

"It looks like it's camouflaged to hide on that coral," Carlos said.

"That's right," said the Friz. "This slug is orange because it's on orange coral. But when the same kind of slug lives on black coral, it's black!"

The sea slug looked really cool. I couldn't wait to tell my aunt Joanne all about it — if we made it back in time.

"What about that one?" said Ralphie. "What kind of coral does that sea slug live on?"

He was pointing at a slug that looked very different. This one wasn't camouflaged at all. In fact, it was so brightly colored that it stood out like a neon sign. Bold white and dark-blue patches covered its body, which was ringed with bright orange. The slug even had bright orange antennae sticking out of its head.

"That one doesn't need camouflage because it's poisonous," said Ms. Frizzle. "Its bright colors are like a sign warning predators not to eat it or they'll get sick."

"Is that why so many of the fish here have such bright colors? To show they're poisonous?" Ralphie asked. The colorful fish around me suddenly didn't look so cute and harmless.

"No, Ralphie. Most fish aren't poisonous at all. Their bright colors are to attract mates," she said. I gave a sigh of relief and bubbles came out of my mouth.

"So none of these fish are poisonous? That's good news, for a change," said Arnold.

"I didn't say *none* of them are poisonous," said Ms. Frizzle. "See that funny-looking fish over there? Don't get too close to that one!"

We cautiously huddled behind Ms. Frizzle.

"What is it?" I asked. I peered at the strange, football-shaped fish, which was covered with spots. The other fish seemed to be staying away from it.

"It's a shame we can't go any closer," Ms. Frizzle said. Then her face lit up. "But we can! Back inside the bus, kids. You're about to see a freckled porcupine fish in a tizzy!"

◄◄►CHAPTER 6◄◄►

The familiar walls of the Magic School Fish suddenly appeared around us. I was relieved to find myself changed from a fish back into a person again. It seemed much safer.

Swimming around the reef was fun, but I was beginning to wonder if we were going to get back to school in time for the assembly. All those people were going to be there waiting for us, including my aunt Joanne.

"Watch closely, kids," Ms. Frizzle called. "We're going to get a rise out of that porcupine fish!"

Our bus-fish was now much bigger than the porcupine fish, so I expected it to swim away when it saw us coming toward it. Instead, it turned to face us, as if challenging us.

"Why bother it?" Arnold said. "Can't we just be friends?"

"Look!" Ms. Frizzle said. When we got so close that we could look into its black, beady eyes, the fish started to puff up. It swelled bigger and bigger, until it had gone from football-shaped to basketball-shaped.

Even weirder, its whole body was now

covered with sharp spines. I hadn't noticed them at first because before the fish saw us, its spines were lying flat. But when we came closer, it stuck its spines straight out.

"Wow!" I said, pulling out my notebook. "I have to draw that for our book!" I sketched it quickly — once puffed and once unpuffed.

Now that we were back in the bus again, everyone started drawing pictures of what we had seen. "The Friz was right. Our new book is going to be even better than our old one," Carlos said.

I kept drawing pictures as we moved through the reef, but something was nagging at me. I knew I was still missing one key picture, but I couldn't remember what it looked like.

"Hey," Carlos said. "Where are all the fish going?"

I looked up from my notebook and saw that he was right. All the fish were getting out of there fast. One of the last to leave was a pretty blue-and-yellow-striped angelfish. Just as it darted out from between two branching pieces of coral, a huge net swept down and scooped it up.

"Look out!" Phoebe screamed.

Before Ms. Frizzle could react, the net came swooping down again.

This time, it was coming right for us.

◄▮►CHAPTER 7◄▮►

Ms. Frizzle tried to steer the Magic School Fish the other way, but the net swooped down so fast that we couldn't escape. We were caught!

"What's going on?" cried Phoebe.

"Somebody must be catching tropical fish — probably to sell for aquariums," Ms. Frizzle said. The bus-fish struggled with all its strength, but its fins were tangled helplessly in the net. We were being dragged upward.

"I don't want to live in somebody's aquarium!" Arnold screamed. "Help!"

"Isn't there something we can do,

Ms. Frizzle?" I asked. I wasn't too crazy about becoming somebody's pet, either.

"Don't worry, kids. The Magic School Bus still has a few tricks left," the Friz said. With the push of a button, the bus-fish's jaws opened, and a pair of scissors came out.

"Hurray!" we all yelled, as the scissors snipped through the net. When we had cut ourselves free, the bus-fish dropped into the water and sped away.

But we weren't out of danger yet. Around us we could see more nets scooping up all the prettiest fish.

"I think it's time to use a little camouflage ourselves," Ms. Frizzle announced. The bus-fish parked next to some staghorn coral and started changing color until we were an exact match for the pinkish coral around us. We looked so much like the coral that a school of small fish swam over and hid behind us.

"Why are those people doing this?" Wanda asked. "Why don't they just leave the poor fish alone?"

"They do it because people pay them to,"

Ms. Frizzle said. "The fish in the fish store have to come from somewhere. And this is where a lot of them come from. Others, like the fish in our classroom, were born to be pets."

"But isn't the fishing bad for the reefs?" Ralphie asked.

"Yes, it is. Collecting is a very big problem," said the Friz. "Just look around you."

The part of the reef where we were hiding looked much less healthy than the place we had been before. A lot of the coral looked dead, and most of it was covered with fuzzy green algae. "When you take away the fish, the whole reef suffers," the Friz said. "With no fish around to eat the algae, it grows out of control. Too much algae smothers the coral and kills it."

"But why is it so much worse over here?" I asked.

"The area where we were before is part of a marine preserve," Ms. Frizzle said. "It's like a national park, only underwater. In protected parts of the park, fishing is banned. We must have crossed the line and gone outside the preserve."

"Thank goodness for the preserve," Keesha said. "Imagine if the whole reef looked just like this!"

"Many coral reefs that aren't protected do look like this," said the Friz.

"But what do the collectors do when they ban fishing?" Ralphie asked.

"That's a good question, Ralphie. In many countries, catching reef fish is an important source of money," Ms. Frizzle said. "But in the long run, protecting reefs actually improves fishing. Fish need a safe place to breed. New fish born in the marine preserve can leave and restock nearby areas. If fishing was legal everywhere, soon there would be no fish left. So protecting reefs can mean more fish to catch, not less. And not only that, marine preserves also bring in money from tourists who come to see healthy reefs."

"So if reefs are protected, everybody wins," Keesha said.

"That's right," said the Friz. "Coral reefs

are home to an incredibly rich variety of plants and animals. If we're not careful, much of this diversity could be gone in the next few decades."

"Gone? Just from fishing?" Carlos said.

"Unfortunately, fishing isn't the only threat. It's not even the main threat," Ms. Frizzle said.

"According to my research," D.A. said, "pollution and global warming are bigger dangers. Even tourists who love coral reefs can accidentally break corals, just by swimming around near them. Do you see that big brain coral over there?"

She pointed to a beautiful, round brain coral about five feet across. A big chunk was missing from one side. "A boat can smash corals like that just by dropping anchor."

"I guess this just shows how important it is to respect how everything in nature works together," D.A. said.

"That's right," Ms Frizzle agreed. "It's important not to disrupt nature's balance."

Coral Reefs in Danger
by Dorothy Ann

Here are some of the major threats to coral reefs:

1. Overfishing
2. Pollution
3. Collecting coral
4. Changes to the environment

To my relief, the bus-fish swam back to a healthier area.

"Ms. Frizzle," Arnold asked, "shouldn't we be going home soon? It's starting to get dark."

"And we need to get back for the assembly," I added.

"Not just yet. Night is when things get really interesting on the reef," the Friz said. "Check out what's happening to the corals."

She switched on the bus-fish's headlights. I sighed. Ms. Frizzle didn't seem worried that we'd miss the assembly, but I knew my aunt Joanne would be disappointed. At least I'd still have lots of great stories to tell her. I sat up straighter and looked out the window so I wouldn't miss a thing.

All around us, corals were slowly unfurling their tentacles. The little bumps we had seen on the hard corals during the day were opening into clusters of little stalks.

"Each ring of tentacles is a coral polyp," Ms. Frizzle said. "At night, they fill themselves with water and inflate to look like blossoms."

"Why?" Wanda asked.

"To catch plankton," the Friz answered.

"Even the ones that get food from algae living inside them?" Ralphie asked.

"Yup," said the Friz. "Those corals get most of their energy from the algae. But hunting provides other important nutrients they need."

"According to my research, some soft

corals live in water almost a mile deep, where it's pitch black!" D.A. said. "Those corals must have to catch all their food, since there's no light."

"That's right." Ms. Frizzle nodded. "But not much plankton lives down there, either. Deep corals mostly collect bits of food called sea snow that sink to the bottom."

"Look! A feather star!" Ralphie interrupted. "I did a report on those." He pointed to a big tangle of arms stretched out like a net.

"I was wondering why we hadn't seen any yet," Ralphie said. "It must have been all rolled up during the day." He started drawing happily in the dim light. It had gotten so dark outside that Ms. Frizzle shone the bus-fish's headlights on the coral until he finished his report.

Feather Stars
by Ralphie

The feather star is an animal related to a starfish. But it has arms that branch and branch again, making it look more like a bush than a starfish.

During the day, a feather star rolls up into a ball. But at night, it spreads out its arms like a big net to catch plankton.

Unlike corals, feather stars aren't stuck in one place. If they're not catching anything in one spot, they just walk somewhere else.

In the distance, I saw some flashing lights. "Ms. Frizzle?" I said. "I think we have company."

"Yikes!" Arnold said. "There's somebody else down here!"

"Oh, boy! Those are flashlight fish," said the Friz.

"Those fish carry flashlights?" Carlos said skeptically.

"No — the light is coming from their bodies," Ms. Frizzle said. "Lots of ocean animals glow, like fireflies do on land. Flashlight fish have two organs below their eyes filled with glowing bacteria. But what makes them really special is that they can blink their lamps on and off, by covering them with a flap of skin like an eyelid."

She steered the bus-fish over to where the flashlight fish were blinking their ghostly green lights. "We'll follow one and see what happens."

The lights moved to the right, so we turned right. But suddenly, the fish were gone. "Hey — how'd they get way over there?" Carlos said, pointing to our left.

"It's a trick," said the Friz. "To escape predators, flashlight fish go one way with their lights on. Then they turn them off and swim back the other way."

"Wow — those fish are really *bright!*" said Carlos. "You might even say they're *brilliant.*"

"Very funny, Carlos," Phoebe said.

"Ms. Frizzle? When you said predators, what did you mean, exactly?" asked Arnold.

"Oh, sharks, rays — a lot of hunters come out at night," the Friz said cheerfully.

Arnold groaned.

"But why at night?" I asked. "Isn't it easier for small fish to hide when it's dark?"

"Lots of hunters find their victims by smell, so darkness doesn't matter," said the Friz. "But some fish have ways to fool them. Look at that!" She shone the bus-fish's headlights on what looked like a slimy plastic bag. "That's a parrot fish. Each night, it makes a bag of mucus around itself."

"What's mucus?" Arnold asked.

"It's like snot," Carlos said.

"Sorry I asked," said Arnold.

"That mucus bag won't protect it if a hunter tries to bite it," said Ms. Frizzle, "but most predators will go right by that parrot fish because they can't smell it through all that mucus."

The thought of sharks and other predators prowling around us in the darkness was starting to creep me out. When I looked out

the windows of the Magic School Fish, I was sure every dark shape I saw was another hungry shark passing by. I tried not to think about it. Besides, we would be leaving soon to go back for the assembly and I knew there was one more drawing I wanted to make before we left. Something good — I just couldn't remember what it was.

By now, the bus headlights were the only thing lighting up the gloom. The reef was getting more and more spooky. We were getting more and more fidgety. Only Ms. Frizzle was humming cheerfully to herself as she steered.

A flat square shape rippled under us, like a blanket blowing in the wind. I shivered.

"That's a ray, class," Ms. Frizzle said. "They're closely related to sharks. That ray can hunt without using either sight *or* smell! It has an extra sense that we don't have: It senses electric fields."

"What good is that?" Carlos said. "There's no electricity down here."

"Actually, there is," said Ms. Frizzle. "All living things generate tiny electric fields with every movement — and every heartbeat. So even animals that bury themselves in the sand can't hide from the ray."

Suddenly, the ray dipped its head and dug into the ocean floor, kicking up a cloud of sand. There was a flurry of activity. "It found something!" the Friz said.

I shivered again. A coral reef didn't seem very safe at night, at least if you were a small animal trying to avoid predators.

"Shouldn't we be going soon?" Phoebe said. "We still have to give our report tonight!"

"There's one very special thing I want to show you first," the Friz said. "Tim, I think you'll be especially interested in this. Did any of you notice the moon tonight?"

I wondered what the Friz was getting at.

"Is that what you wanted to show us?" Carlos asked doubtfully. "The moon?"

"No. But it's actually exactly three days after the full moon. Does anyone know what that means at this time of the year?" Ms. Frizzle asked.

Suddenly, I remembered what my missing report was about. "Yes!" I said. "Is it really happening tonight?"

"That's right, Tim! Tonight is the night!" Ms. Frizzle said.

"Hurray!" I said. "I can't believe it! One night out of the whole year, and we're going to see it!"

"What? What are we going to see?" everybody shouted.

"Go ahead, tell them, Tim," the Friz said with a grin.

"You know how corals are rooted in place?" I said. "That makes it impossible for them to go out and find mates. So to reproduce, female corals send millions of eggs out into the water. At the same time, the male corals send out seeds to fertilize them."

"What do you mean, 'fertilize them'?" asked Wanda.

"The male and female cells combine to

make new coral larvae. Each new larva swims around for a while, then settles on the bottom of the ocean to start a new colony."

Coral Babies

by Tim

Corals make more coral in two different ways.

One way is by cloning. To do this, a coral polyp just splits into two polyps. Eventually, the polyp clones spread out into a whole colony.

The other way is for one coral to release eggs, which are fertilized by another coral. The fertilized eggs become tiny larvae that settle down and create whole new colonies.

"But how can they be sure the eggs and seeds will meet in the water and get fertilized?" Phoebe asked.

"Most of them don't," I said. "That's why corals send out so many eggs. A lot get washed out to sea. And a whole lot get eaten by other animals. Remember those sea fans and anemones, with their webs and tentacles for catching plankton? They eat a lot of the eggs. So do other animals, like small fish. So to make sure some survive, corals send out millions of eggs at a time."

"Is that what's happening tonight?" Carlos asked.

"Yeah. Some animals spawn, or release eggs, a few at a time," I said. "But corals send out their eggs and seeds all at once. That increases the chances they will mix and fertilize. With millions of eggs in the water at a certain time, there's no way that they can all be eaten."

"It's called synchronized spawning," Ms. Frizzle added. "Synchronized just means at the same time. And that time is now!"

I looked out the window at where the headlights were shining on some hard corals. Hundreds of little eggs were slowly rising up

from it. They were barely the size of the head of a pin.

All around us, the same thing was happening. It looked like a snowstorm, only upside down because instead of falling, the snow was rising upward.

"It looks like a blizzard!" said Wanda.

More and more eggs were coming out of the corals until it looked like the water was full of drifting snow. It was beautiful. I whipped out my notebook and started to draw.

While the class oohed and aahed like they were watching fireworks, I finished my last report. The first time I'd drawn it, I hadn't known enough to make a good picture. But now it was going to be my best picture of all. I couldn't wait to show it to the whole school, and especially to my aunt Joanne — that is, if we weren't too late.

I drew a picture of everything I could see in the night scene before me: branching staghorn coral, lumpy brain coral, big frilly sea fans, and, through it all, millions of tiny coral eggs. It looked like something from a fairy tale.

"Fasten your seat belts, everyone," Ms. Frizzle announced. "We're heading home."

I grinned. We were on our way back! With luck, we just might make it in time for the assembly, and our new book of reports was going to be even better than our last one. I couldn't wait to show it to my aunt.

I closed my notebook, yawned, and settled into my seat. It had been a long day.

The bus floated up to the surface, then sprouted wings and took off. Within five minutes, I was sound asleep.

ᐊᐁᐧᐳ**CHAPTER 8**ᐊᐁᐧᐳ

Back at school, everyone worked really hard to put the finishing touches on our new book. It came out even better than the first one because we were drawing and writing about things we had actually seen. And my new picture of the corals spawning at night was on the front cover.

At last it was time for our big presentation.

First Wanda gave her report on farmer fish. Everyone was amazed to learn that fish raise crops for food, just like people do. Then Arnold gave his report on camouflage. Everybody loved his imitation of a stonefish pouncing from a pile of rocks.

Next Ralphie told everyone about how feather stars unfurl at night, which he demonstrated with his arms, and Dorothy Ann told everyone about all the ways pollution threatens corals.

The whole auditorium was completely absorbed as the rest of the class read their reports and showed their drawings. It was like our presentation was letting everybody share in our incredible trip.

Finally, I told everyone about how corals release their eggs all at once and described how amazing everything looks on the reef at night. Then I held up my pictures. Everyone clapped for a really long time. I could see my aunt Joanne beaming at me from the audience, right next to my parents. They all looked really proud.

When the assembly was over, Ms. Frizzle let me hold the book and show it to my family. I was especially excited to hear what my aunt would have to say.

She flipped through the book for a long time, looking at every page carefully. Finally, I

couldn't wait any longer. "Well?" I said. "What do you think?"

"I'm — I'm amazed," she said. "These pictures are incredible. They're so realistic, you'd think your class had actually visited a coral reef. But of course that's impossible."

"Of course," I said with a grin. I winked at Ms. Frizzle and returned Aunt Joanne's hug. It had been a great day.

The Magic School Bus®

science CHAPTER BOOKS

Hop on the Magic School Bus for out-of-this-world adventure!

At bookstores everywhere!

Scholastic Inc., P.O. Box 7502, Jefferson City, MO 65102

Please send me the books I have checked above. I am enclosing $_____ (please add $2.00 to cover shipping and handling). Send check or money order—no cash or C.O.D.s please.

Name_____ Birth date_____

Address_____

City_____ State/Zip_____

Please allow four to six weeks for delivery. Offer good in U.S.A. only. Sorry, mail orders are not available to residents of Canada. Prices subject to change.

◧ SCHOLASTIC

MSBBKLST0504